Curious George's
Big Book of
Curiosity

Illustrated in the style of H. A. Rey by Greg Paprocki

Houghton Mifflin Company

Boston 2005

Copyright © 2005 by Houghton Mifflin Company

Curious George® is a registered trademark of Houghton Mifflin Company.

All rights reserved. For information about permission to reproduce selections
from this book, write to Permissions, Houghton Mifflin Company, 215 Park
Avenue South, New York, New York 10003.

www.houghtonmifflinbooks.com

The text of this book is set in New Century Schoolbook.
The illustrations are watercolor, pencil, and charcoal.

Illustrated by Greg Paprocki
Designed by Sue Dennen

Library of Congress Cataloging-in-Publication Data

Margret & H. A. Rey's Curious George's big book of curiosity / illustrated in the
style of H. A. Rey by Greg Paprocki.
    p. cm.
   ISBN 0-618-58338-6 (hardcover)
   1. Vocabulary—Juvenile literature. 2. Curious George (Fictitious character)—
Juvenile literature. I. Title: Curious George's big book of curiosity. II. Title:
Curious George's big book of curiosity. III. Rey, Margret. IV. Rey, H. A. (Hans
Augusto), 1898–1977. V. Paprocki, Greg, ill.
   PE1449.M365 2005
   428.1'3—dc22
                                                                    2005003167

ISBN-13: 978-0618-58338-6

Printed in China
SCP 10 9 8 7 6 5 4 3 2 1

This is George.

He is a good little monkey
and always very curious.

Let's see what George is curious about today…

Parts of the Body

hair

head

ears

teeth

arms

fingers

elbow

hands

eyes

nose

mouth

legs

back

bottom

belly

knees

toes

feet

Emotions Sometimes I feel...

surprised

scared

sad

sleepy

angry

happy

sister

brother

father

mother

grandparents

friend

Family

uncle

aunt

friend

cousins

pet

friends

Clothing

shirt

underpants

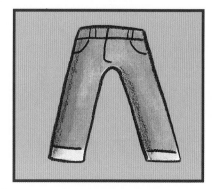

pants

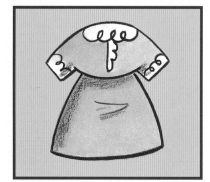

dress

jacket

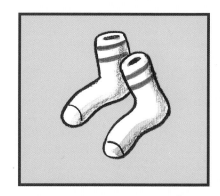

socks

sneakers

hat

Toys

puppets

kite

rocking horse

ball

tool set

bubbles

dolls

blocks

cards

paints

train set

crayons

clay

puzzle

yo-yo

robots

marbles

Your Neighborhood

Jobs

librarian

teacher

police officer

astronaut

firefighters

farmer

lifeguard

carpenter

nurse

scientist

magician

rock star

doctor

janitor

dancer

fisherman

baker

soldier

pilot

veterinarian

store clerk

writer

artist

athlete

hairdresser

letter carrier

Home Sweet Home

house

tree house

igloo

castle

skyscraper

hut

cabin

trailer

pueblo

houseboat

birdhouse

apartment

Where's George?

steak

chicken

cheese

cash register

shopping cart

bread

EXIT

Meals

Breakfast

pancakes

jelly

toast

eggs and bacon

juice

cereal

Lunch

apple

veggies

milk

sandwiches

pizza

carrot sticks

potato chips

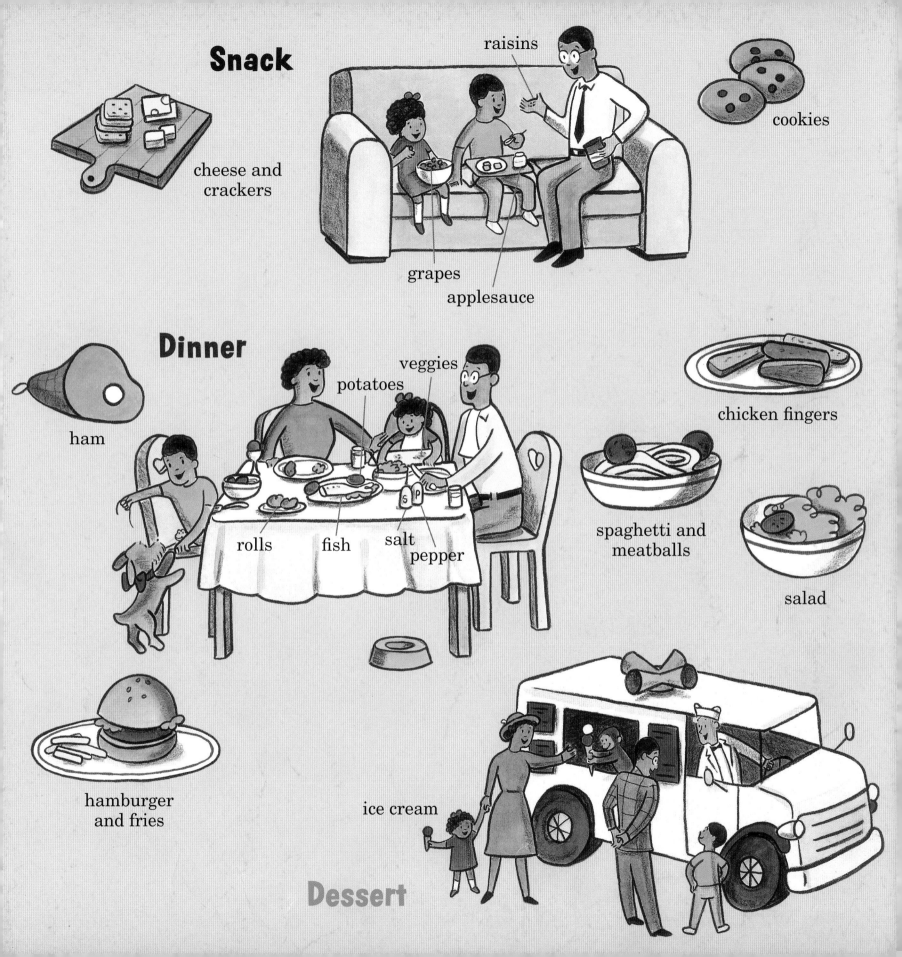

Snack

cheese and crackers

raisins

cookies

grapes

applesauce

Dinner

ham

veggies

potatoes

chicken fingers

rolls

fish

salt

pepper

spaghetti and meatballs

salad

hamburger and fries

ice cream

Dessert

On the Go

ice cream truck

bus

cars

plane

boats

train

scooter

bike

submarine

hot air balloon

rocket

tricycle

wagon

roller skates

motorcycle

trucks

unicycle

baby carriage

taxi

tractor

Farm Animals and Sounds

farmhouse

field

cock-a-doodle-doo

cat

meow

rooster

fence

cluck cluck

chicken

oink

pigs

chick

peep

baaaa

sheep

Counting

1 whale

2 elephants

3 rhinos

4 hippos

5 giraffes

6 camels

7 bears

8 lions

9 ostriches

10 kangaroos

11 zebra

12 seals

13 monkeys

14 penguins

15 dogs

16 cats

17 rabbits

18 turtles

19 hedgehogs

20 frogs

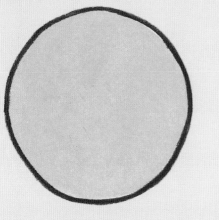

circle

square

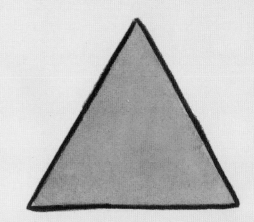

triangle

diamond

Shapes

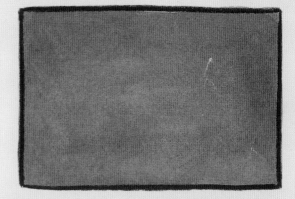

rectangle

oval

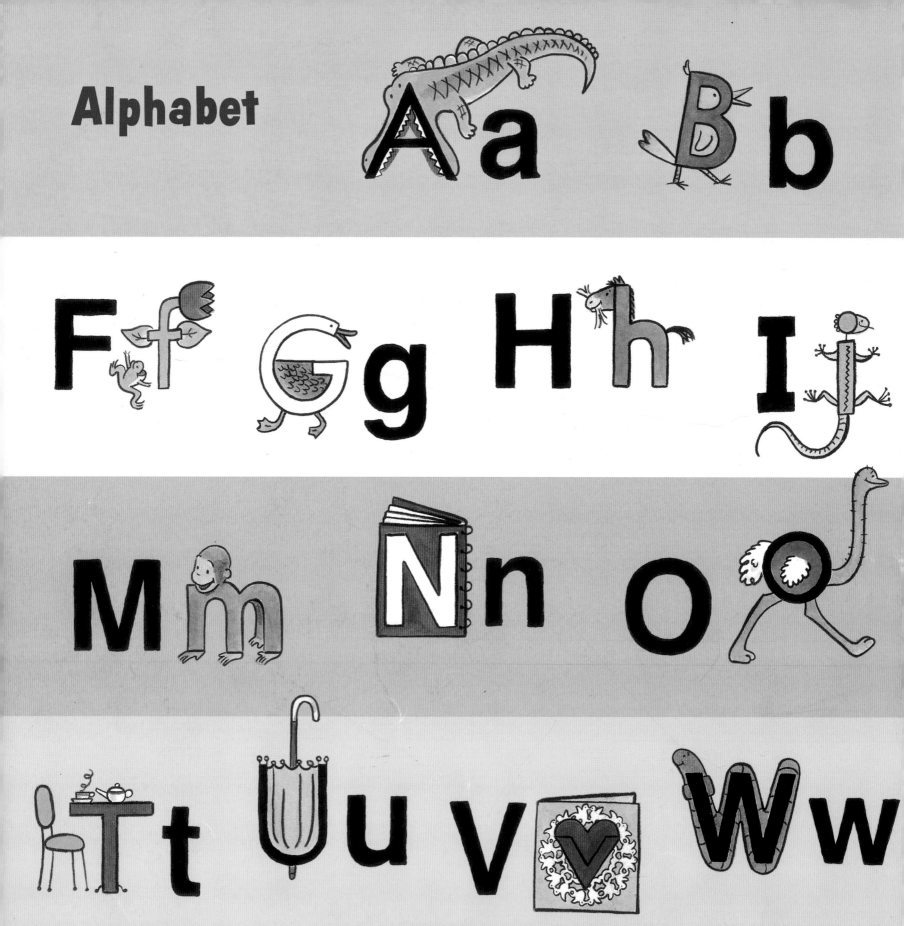

Alphabet

A a B b

F f G g H h I i

M m N n O o

T t U u V v W w

C c

D d

E e

J j

K k

L l

P p

Q q

R r

S s

X x

Y y

Z z

Opposites

up   down

smile   frown

hot   cold

new   old

empty   full

push   pull

short   tall

big   small

stop

go

fast

slow

out

in

fat

thin

above

below

goodbye

hello

Superlatives

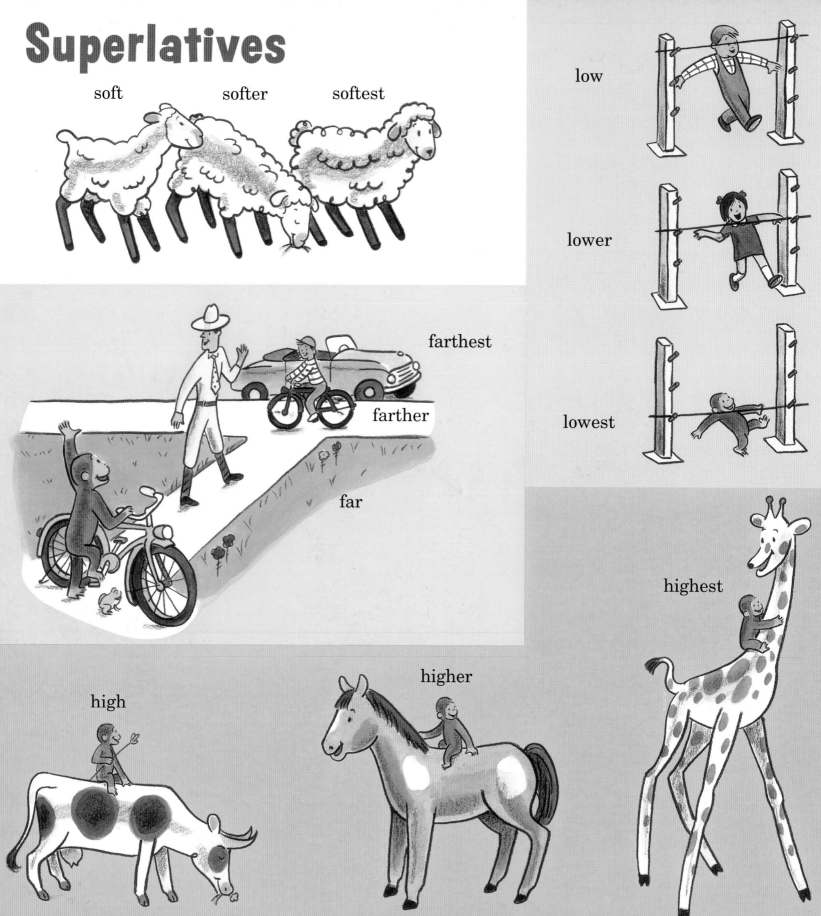

soft   softer   softest

low

lower

lowest

farthest

farther

far

highest

high   higher

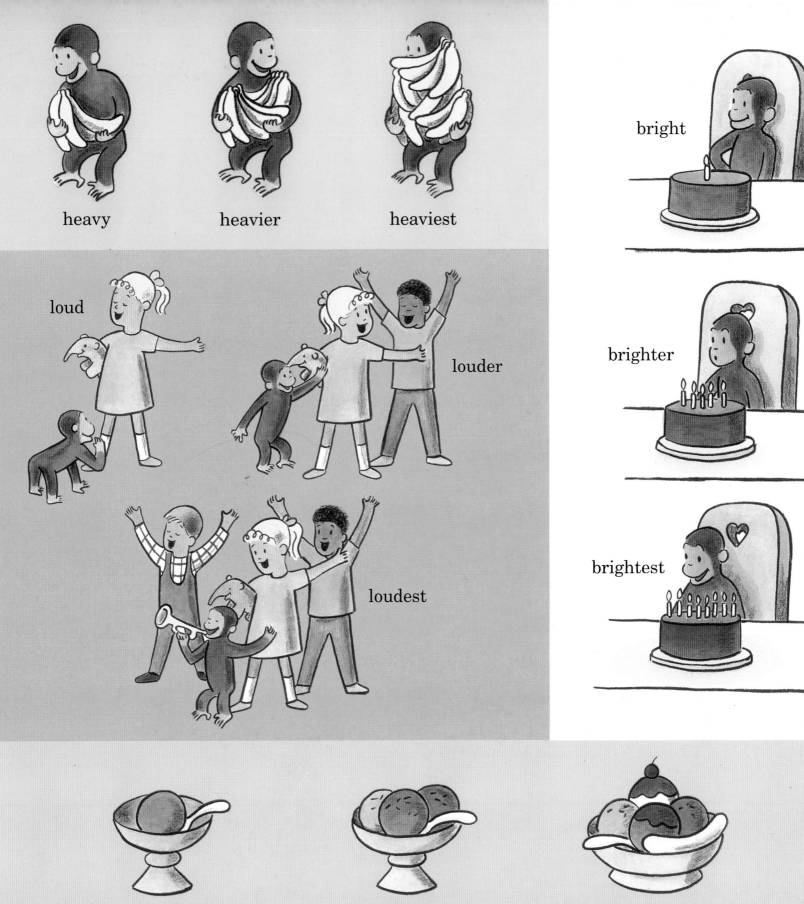

heavy   heavier   heaviest

loud   louder   loudest

bright   brighter   brightest

tasty   tastier   tastiest!

Seasons
Winter

icicles

snowflakes

skis

scarf

mittens

hat

snowman

snowsuit

hot chocolate

snowshoes

sled

ice skates

snow

Spring

raincoat

rain

birds

grass

galoshes

mud

umbrella

sprouts

spring flowers

seeds

Summer

sunglasses
sun umbrella
swimsuit
sandcastle
sand
seagulls
beach chair
water wings
flip-flops
sunscreen
shovel
pail
crab
seashells
seaweed
ocean

Fall

shed
scarecrow
cider
apples
pumpkins
sweater
leaves
rake

Weather

sun

rain

snow

thunder and lightning

wind

fog

rainbow

clouds

Colors

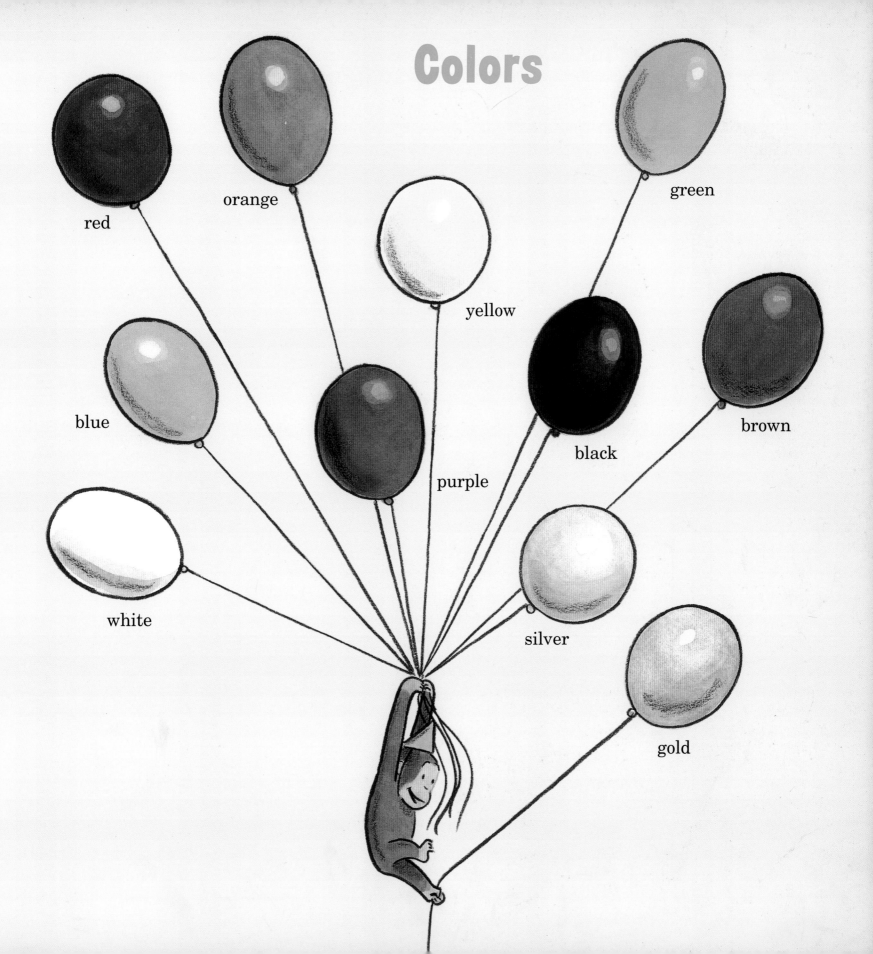

red

orange

green

yellow

blue

purple

black

brown

white

silver

gold

Pets

ant farm

parakeet

dog

puppy

hamster

Pet Show & Tell

$4 + 1 = 5$

kitten

turtle

ferret

fish

rabbit

lizard

Playground

jungle gym

slide

tire swing

seesaw

sandbox

jump rope

hopscotch

tricycle

violin

guitar

Musical Instruments

cymbals

tuba

flute

trumpet

bandleader

trombone

drums

xylophone

Your World

moon

stars

ocean

desert

Bath Time

mirror

towel

toothbrush
toothpaste

shampoo

soap

bathrobe

sink

rubber
duckie

slippers

comb

hairbrush

tub

toilet

clothes
hamper

Bedtime

curtains

poster

clock

bed

lamp

night-light

pajamas

blanket

teddy
bear

bedtime
story

friends

blocks

toys

The End